THE
GHOSTLY TALES
OF
ST. AUGUSTINE
&
ST. JOHNS COUNTY

Published by Arcadia Children's Books
A Division of Arcadia Publishing
Charleston, SC
www.arcadiapublishing.com

Spooky America is a trademark of Arcadia Publishing, Inc.

First published 2021

Manufactured in the United States

ISBN 978-1-4671-9832-5

Library of Congress Control Number: 2021938391

Notice: The information in this book is true and complete to the best of our knowledge. It is offered without guarantee on the part of the author or Arcadia Publishing. The author and Arcadia Publishing disclaim all liability in connection with the use of this book.

All images courtesy of Shutterstock.com; p. 32 Dale Taylor/Shutterstock.com; p. 44 Rosemarie Mosteller/Shutterstock.com; p. 54 Editorial credit: Felix Mizioznikov/Shutterstock.com; p.72 Sandra Foyt/Shutterstock.com.

Spooky America

THE GHOSTLY TALES OF ST. AUGUSTINE & ST. JOHNS COUNTY

JESSA DEAN

Adapted from *Haunted St. Augustine and St. Johns County* by Elizabeth Randall

arcadia
CHILDREN'S BOOKS

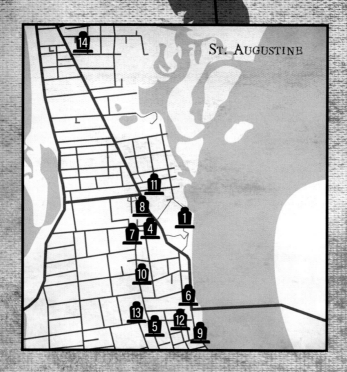

SOUTH
CAROLINA

GEORGIA

ALABAMA

ATLANTIC OCEAN

FLORIDA ③ 〇 ⑮ ②

ST. AUGUSTINE

⑭

⑪
⑧
⑦ ④ ①
⑩
⑥
⑬ ⑫
⑤ ⑨

TABLE OF CONTENTS & MAP KEY

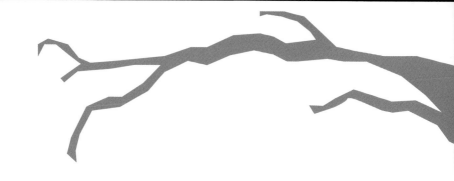

Introduction

One thing you'll figure out quickly while walking the cobblestone streets of St. Augustine is that it is 100 percent haunted. Ghosts are among the perks of being in the oldest city in the United States. In fact, I'd be surprised if you *didn't* see a ghost or five during your visit there.

You'll need all the ghost-finding courage you can get when visiting St. Augustine and the area around it, St. Johns County. This county has bragging rights to some of the most historic sites in America. That much history comes with lots of old, dead bones and the spirits who left them. Sure, you'll find the dead buried in a couple of local cemeteries. But there are just as many, if not more, buried under the stones of streets you walk on. That leaves plenty of room for surprise encounters with the supernatural.

Before the British colonies and the American Revolution, St. Augustine was a thriving Spanish settlement. Traces of the Spanish outpost and of the earlier Native American village still linger for you to explore. The city is as full of ghosts as tourists, and many places you'll visit have tales of murder and mayhem to tell. There are old forts where bloody battles left men to rot under the hot sun. Hotels in the area have stories of guests who didn't make it out alive. You may feel a chill run up your spine while you eat fried shrimp for dinner at a local restaurant. In St. Augustine, you have to wonder if the floor you're walking on sits on top of an ancient Native American burial ground. The city officials didn't exactly consult the dead before they started building.

At certain times of the night, as the mist rolls in and the trees turn dark in the moonlight, the dead make themselves known. You might find yourself wishing you'd stayed at your hotel. But if the ghosts want to say hello, walls won't keep them out. You never know who or what you'll stumble upon in St. Augustine, so it's best to have a guide show you the way. If you're up for the journey, grab your flashlight and your video camera. Let's go hunt us some ghosts.

You can handle it, right?

Castillo de San Marcos National Monument

Defending the Dead

What would you say if I told you there's a place where the walls echo with ancient cannon fire, there's a pit of quicksand that was used to dispose of dead bodies, and headless ghosts roam the grounds? Interested? Well, read on, because one of the most haunted places in St. Augustine is also one of the most interesting places.

Echoes of the dead show up frequently at the Castillo de San Marcos. This fortress was built by the Spanish to defend the coast from the British, and it did its job well. So many people died there in so many ways that we don't even know how many people were buried there. That means, of course, we also don't know exactly how many ghosts still haunt the grounds.

Imagine you're a soldier in the Spanish army, stationed at the Castillo. The British ships are in the bay, and you can see them loading up the cannons. Your buddies are taking up positions around the fort, ready to defend St. Augustine. The smell of gun smoke and sweat lingers in the air. The sun beats down on the back of your neck in the space

between your helmet and your armor. You stand on the parapet of the fort, watching and waiting, nerves firing and mind racing. Will this be your last battle?

It sounds like something out of a movie: a huge fortress of stone, complete with dungeons and a moat built to support an entire town during a siege by the enemy. But the Castillo, also known as Fort Marion, was a real part of American history. The stone walls shook with cannon fire. Prisoners rotted in the dungeons. The fort even had a room for torturing captured soldiers. But I bet you're waiting to hear about the quicksand.

For a long time, no one knew about this secret feature of the fort. It had been sealed off for years and was found by accident when the roof was damaged. The torture room was hard to get into, with an opening only about three-feet high or about half the height of a tall man. It had no windows. The stone walls here are thicker than anywhere else in the fort, probably to muffle the screams as people were tortured. The soldiers used several different devices to punish prisoners who would not spill their battle secrets. Then when the prisoners died, the quicksand waited for them.

In the corner of a room was a large hole, much wider and deeper than a man's body. Soldiers could shove dead bodies into the hole

into the quicksand underneath. Quicksand looks solid, but it's really made of liquified sand or clay. It would hold the body in place until either the tide came in and took the body with it or the body decomposed. Their bones could have ended up anywhere, but their spirits certainly remained at the Castillo. They roam the grounds with others who died there, whispering to anyone who will listen. During the day, they're harder to hear, but they're there.

You probably wouldn't want to stick around too long after dark at the Castillo. You might be overwhelmed by the number of ghosts because the torture room wasn't the only place people died. The dungeons proved just as deadly. Prisoners were kept there for long periods of time. The Spanish took land from the Native American tribes in the area, so many tribe members ended up there. Seminole Chief Osceola remains here, at least in spirit. His image appears on the wall outside the dungeon where he was kept. Many people report seeing him clearly. If you get a chance to visit the dungeons, keep an eye out for him.

The chief isn't the only spirit trapped in the walls of the Castillo. When you're walking around the fort, you may smell perfume in a particular spot, even if no one is around. It's said the perfume was worn by a woman who was walled up into the fort by her husband. That's right, he put her inside while she was still alive and closed up the wall behind her. No wonder she still haunts the fortress, probably searching for a way out! At the Castillo, there was only one way in or out, though, and most didn't make it out.

Over the years, it became clear that many more people died inside the Castillo and on the grounds than had been recorded. In fact, in the 1800s workers found a pile of skeletons inside an underground dungeon no one knew about. Were these captured British soldiers who wasted away in the dungeon? Or were they Spanish soldiers who died during battle and were stored there until they could be properly buried but then forgotten? No one knows.

When the Castillo was built, the Spanish built it right on the water to make sure they could protect themselves against Britain's superior fleet. But the British navy was strong, and their cannons did a lot of damage. The fort stayed pretty intact because it was made from coquina (a building material made from shells) that protected it from the shock. But the human body is no match for a cannon, and many soldiers lost their heads instantly.

One of these headless soldiers still wanders the grounds outside the fort. You might assume he's looking for his head, but he's not. Instead, he desperately searches for a lost wedding ring. Was he waiting to get home to his wife after the battle? Or was he planning to ask his girl to marry him when he'd completed his service? The ring has long disappeared, of course, but maybe you can point out a spot to search if you run into him. He's been looking for a long time.

If you visit the Castillo today, you'll see employees in costumes reenacting the conflicts with Britain. The cannons even point out at Matanzas Bay, as if waiting for the British show up. The only explosions most will hear are fireworks when both locals and tourists come to the Castillo grounds for a big Fourth of July celebration. But put your ear against the fort's walls. Can you hear the thunderous booms of cannons? Can you hear the echoes of soldiers in the heat of battle, calling out orders as they defended the fort?

Will you experience something supernatural at the Castillo de San Marcos? Probably. But if you need directions to the nearest ghost, you might want to ask one of your fellow travelers. The park rangers who work there will probably glare at you. They're not so fond of the supernatural.

As for other fortresses in St. Augustine, you won't hear as many ghost stories about them. But with all the battles that took place within their walls, ghosts are a given. They're harder to find, but they're lurking around, just waiting for a real ghost hunter like you.

Fort Matanzas conjures up the image of vengeful ghosts. After all, the word *Matanzas* means "killings" or "slaughter" in Spanish. There was a huge massacre of French Huguenot soldiers by the Spanish here. But the ghosts here are actually pretty quiet most of the time.

The fort is run by the same people who run the Castillo, so no one's going to help you find the ghosts. You'll have to search for them. Those who've sought them out spot their uniforms first. Both French and Spanish soldiers roam the old fort. You might even get lucky and hear their footsteps on the stone floors like others have.

Like Fort Matanzas, Fort Mose was also the site of a bloody battle. Native American militia and freed African slaves led a battle against the British. In fact, Fort Mose was a black settlement before the Spanish gave up Florida.

Nothing of the fort remains aboveground, but you can still visit and walk the forty-two acres where the settlement existed. It's a little tricky to find ghosts without a building, but they roam the fields just the same. Keep your eyes open and your ears alert. Listen for their whispers. They'll appear to you if they know you're looking for them.

You might have to go on your own to find a good ghostly encounter at the forts, but you'll be an expert in ghost hunting by the time we're done here.

Old City Gates

A Ghostly Welcome

The Castillo played the main role in St. Augustine's defense, but the city gates did, too. In the past, they marked the entrance to the city, but these days, they're the site of a frequent ghost sighting. Let's dive into the story of one of St. Augustine's most often-spotted spirits: a woman in white.

If you've been a ghost hunter for long, you've probably heard of women in white.

These female ghosts roam the countryside—
and sometimes back roads—in white dresses.
Legends of women in white are common
throughout America and even other countries.

Some of these spirits are said to warn people about danger ahead. They appear before winter storms to caution you to stay inside. They stand in the road to protect you from collisions with oncoming cars. Other women in white are said to haunt bad men who have hurt women. Legends tell us they seek revenge on the men because they cannot get revenge on the person who hurt them. There may not be any truth to that, but it's a popular trope in supernatural movies.

It makes sense that St. Augustine would have several "women in white" stories. Before air conditioning and electric fans, women in the South usually wore white during the summer to help beat the heat and humidity. But summer was a bad time for a lot of women. Many of them died in this season from giving birth or from illness, including an epidemic of yellow fever, a deadly virus. A lot of child spirits also can appear in white because it was a common custom to bury them in white clothes.

The first person to die from yellow fever in St. Augustine is also probably the best-known woman in white in town. Elizabeth, who died in 1821, was the teenage daughter of the keeper of the city gates. You'll have to stay up way past your bedtime to catch her. She usually appears around two or three in the morning and stands near the right-end gate toward the center.

She often waves at the cars passing by and dances in front of the gates.

Elizabeth isn't buried at the gates, as you might think. She's buried on Anastacia Island off the coast because her father didn't have the money to bury her in town. But she returns home often to give visitors a clear warning: don't pass the gates, or you'll get yellow fever. Unless you know to look for her, you might not even realize she's a ghost when you see her. People see her long, flowing hair and white lacey dress in the middle of the night, and they call the police thinking she's lost. But really, she's home.

The Ghostly Women of St. Augustine

It's less clear why a woman in white haunts the Casa Monica Hotel, specifically the Ponce de Leon suite (named for the Spanish explorer who first landed in St. Augustine). The woman wears a fancy white dress that appears to be from the 1920s. She paces the suite, even when guests occupy it. Ghost hunters have captured her on film. You might see her if you look up at the windows of the suite from below.

Most say the woman in white is Abbie Brooks, an author and historian whose painting hangs on the third floor of the hotel. Many locals disagree. But what everyone *does* agree on is that Abbie's painting is haunted.

Staff at the hotel are pretty stingy with the details of ghost sightings. But they will tell you all about the painting. Abbie wears a bright-red gown and hat and stands against the backdrop of the front of the hotel. Her eyes look straight at you, until they move. That's right, they follow you as you move up the stairs.

As if that isn't creepy enough, Abbie's spirit doesn't stay in the painting. Abbie doesn't just haunt the Ponce de Leon suite. She likes to mess with people around the hotel. She will follow employees and whisper their names. Guests and staff tell stories of an odd thumping coming from a room above them or someone closing a door over and over again down the hall.

There are no guests in those rooms at the time. Some report hearing running up and down the halls in the middle of the night.

Between 1962 and 1997, the Casa Monica wasn't a hotel. It served as the St. Johns County Courthouse. Instead of guests in fancy clothes having dinner, visitors during that time stood in line to pay speeding tickets. Maybe Abbie liked having the place to herself at night back then and is mad she has to share with hotel guests again.

No one's really sure why Abbie sticks around. She didn't live or die in the hotel, and she's buried at a local cemetery. If you stay at the Casa Monica, maybe you can ask her. At least she's easier to deal with than our next woman in white.

Catalina de Porras drifts through the walls at Harry's

Seafood Bar and Grille wearing a trailing white dress. It makes sense to see her there, since she used to own the building. She mostly haunts the women's restroom, which was once her bedroom. If you look in the mirror while washing your hands, she might say hello. On certain special nights, though, Catalina shows herself to the entire restaurant. Can you imagine taking a bite of fish and seeing her float by you?

If you do encounter Catalina, make sure you're polite. She hates rudeness, especially cursing. Any of the locals will tell you that most

St. Augustine ghosts hate cursing. So if you take a ghost tour, your guide will warn you to watch your words, especially around Catalina.

Some restaurant patrons don't listen. The employees at Harry's tell of one visitor who cursed with every other word. All of a sudden, his head flew back, and his nose started to bleed! Some diners try to coax Catalina into the room by cursing on purpose. But it's not a

good idea. You might not get punched. Some rude visitors have been chased by swarms of flies and had other strange experiences that made them think twice before saying anything!

They're not the only ones to experience the unexplained at Harry's, though. Visit for a meal and you might smell strange odors. You might even get a glimpse of Catalina or another spirit in one of the mirrors or out of the corner of your eye in the doorways.

Whether they appear to visitors with good intentions or not, the women in white of St. Augustine aren't to be messed with! So let's leave them in peace and be on our way to explore some more.

Tolomato Cemetery

Chasing Ghosts and Graves

You're probably not surprised when you hear that a cemetery is haunted. We expect them to be, right? Not everyone rests in peace. But Tolomato Cemetery has more than its share of ghosts, including its own woman in white.

A beautiful bride in a flowing white dress floats above the ground at Tolomato, surrounded by an eerie mist that confuses the eye. No one knows who she is or what she wants.

It's not even clear if she's buried there. Was she abandoned at the altar the night she died? Did her new husband harm her? Where is her groom anyway? She's not talking, and people don't get close enough to ask. But since she's still sticking around, it seems likely something bad happened.

To meet the bride, you can follow a dirt path that leads straight to a big white chapel with a cross on top. A huge tree arches over the path to mark her territory. That's how you'll know you're in the right spot. But be careful, traveler.

Make sure to stay on the path, and don't stray over the stone barriers on either side. If you do, you just might get pulled into a nearby grave! The mist is tricky, and the ghosts don't like to be disturbed. Let's get to know more about the cemetery's residents. Then you'll know whether to consider them friends or foes when you visit.

Tolomato is the oldest planned cemetery in the United States, so you can see why it's full of paranormal activity. Even before the cemetery existed, the land had been a burial ground

since the sixteenth century. The planners had a strict vision of what the cemetery would look like. They even dictated the colors and type of masonry allowed in the cemetery! Forget having some cool sculpture of a hand coming out of a grave or a purple gravestone. The graves needed to look exactly alike and be the same size. Their plans didn't exactly work out like they'd hoped.

Ask a local who knows about the cemetery, and they'll be the first to tell you that the dead don't get much rest there. Hundreds of years of bad weather have made a mark. Wind, floods, storms, and tides have disturbed the final resting place of Tolomato's dead. Extreme weather has made a mess of the cemetery over its long history. Hurricanes flooded the area, leaving coffins floating on the water. High winds stirred up the dirt and long-buried bones. Storm surges from the ocean likely even carried bones from the cemetery to other parts of town. Unmarked graves lie all over St. Augustine, so no one really knows who is actually still buried in Tolomato.

But the weather isn't the worst thing to disturb Tolomato's dead. Bodies have been removed from the cemetery to make room for new ones or snatched for more sinister reasons. Criminals destroyed many of the graves over the years. Some searched for valuables, since families often buried their loved ones with jewelry or other precious items. Others took the bones or even freshly buried bodies to sell to medical schools. One of the first people buried in Tolomato is a known victim of grave robbers. Some men looking for things to sell dug up the grave of a teenage girl. Now she roams the cemetery seeking rest she'll never find.

Can you imagine being a graverobber? First, you'd have to dig up all that dirt covering the casket. At night. With the dead surrounding you. Every noise you hear would have the hair standing up on the back of your neck!

Then if you could move your fingers after that hard work, you'd have to pry open the lid.

The smell would be disgusting. Enough to make you throw up your dinner all over the grave! And just think about pulling out the bones. What if it was a somewhat fresh body and still had some skin and muscle on it? Truly gross. I'd run away, not wrap up the body to take with me!

At one point, a pack of wild dogs even overran the cemetery, and no one could access it. They ruled over their kingdom of the dead, and I'm sure they made off with a few bones!

Grave robbers and wild dog packs aren't common threats to the cemetery these days, but centuries-old trees still watch over the dead. A wire fence protects the cemetery boundary. Many tombs remain above-ground, some with carved headstones and fancy iron fences around them. But a lot of the gravestones are broken or missing. Many markers made from wood eroded a long time ago. Since the cemetery closed to new burials in 1884, you won't see any new graves there. But you just might make friends with a strangely dressed little boy who likes to run around the cemetery.

Five-year-old Jamie Morgan (born James) is the most famous of the ghosts at Tolomato. Not everyone gets to meet him. Readers of this book are in luck since he only appears to kids (sorry to the cool ghost-hunting adults reading this). If you don't see him running and jumping

over graves, look up! Jamie likes to sit in one of the trees, with his legs swinging wildly. But you'll have to make your parents hang out on the other side of the cemetery. He won't come out if adults are present.

No one seems to know how Jamie died. Some people guess it's from falling out of the same tree he likes to climb. You can see his headstone at the front of the cemetery if you're facing west. It has his name, birthday, and date of death—November 28, 1877—ten days after his fifth birthday.

Jamie might even show you around the cemetery, since he's a little lonely. His parents and his brother and sister all died after the cemetery closed, so they're buried somewhere else. After the cemetery closed, some families couldn't bury the recently deceased with their loved ones. But some had creative ways to get around that.

Catalina Usina Llambias died with one final wish: to be buried in Tolomato. But she died too late—two years after the cemetery closed to burials. That didn't stop her son, though. He broke into the cemetery and buried her there anyway. Of course, he was arrested, but the punishment was minimal. The judge yelled at him and made him pay a fine of $25. They didn't even move his mother's body.

How many others buried family members there, late at night under the moon and didn't get caught? Only the ghosts of Tolomato know, and they're not going to give up the cemetery's secrets so easily.

The Huguenot Cemetery

CHAPTER 5

Counting Up the Ghosts

While Tolomato Cemetery has had some rough moments, another of the city's cemeteries remains peaceful and beautiful. Spanish moss hangs down over the graves. Markers made of marble and stone gleam in the sunlight. There are even two crosses carved out of coquina, probably the only ones in the world since coquina usually crumbles when it's carved. The Huguenot Cemetery is locked up tight, so no one can visit without permission...at least, no one *alive*.

The Huguenot Cemetery is supposed to be the most haunted graveyard in St. Augustine. Stand outside the gates at night, and you'll likely experience something strange. In addition to ghosts, people also report seeing lights and floating orbs and hearing weird noises.

But some say the cemetery isn't haunted. They say the coffins remain, but the ghosts left long ago. There are plenty of ghosts elsewhere, so why waste your time hanging around outside a locked-up cemetery? Of course, you and I both know the cemetery is where we want to be! Cemeteries are natural places for ghosts to gather. Fences may not keep ghosts in, but luckily they don't keep ghosts away, either!

Take old Judge John Stickney, for example. He's a well-known figure in St. Augustine history who is no longer buried at the Huguenot Cemetery, but still haunts it. That's right, I said he's not even buried there anymore! His kids dug him up and took him across the country to Washington, DC. A ten-foot-tall marble monument to the judge remains on cemetery grounds, but something else keeps him there. When the gravediggers dug up the judge to move his body, grave robbers swooped in and took his gold teeth. The judge still wanders the cemetery looking for his teeth each night.

The Huguenot Cemetery has always been a popular target for theft and vandalism throughout its long history. That's why it's locked up tight now. In true St. Augustine style, the cemetery even has ghosts to enforce its boundaries. Don't stick your arms through the iron gates at the back of the cemetery unless you want to be grabbed by cold, undead hands. Three men who all died in January 1835 patrol the gates, and they'll try to pull you through to join them.

These three men ranged in age from 23 to 35 and came from New York and Massachusetts. Not much else is known about them, but their identical gravestones show they might have been friends before their deaths. Many visitors to the cemetery have been pinched or poked when they get too close to the gates. If you do get permission to go inside the cemetery, watch out! The men might try to trip or shove you. They might even tap you on the shoulder or knock your hat off.

You might be thinking, "Big deal, some ghosts like to pull pranks." But these three men aren't the spookiest thing about the cemetery. You don't need to fear the spirits we can identify because of their marked gravestones. What you need to fear—what truly sends a chill up the spine—is that there's a whole year of time where countless bodies were buried in the cemetery with no gravestones.

The Huguenot Cemetery was created to handle the many St. Augustine citizens who died from yellow fever, an epidemic that devastated our new country. In 1821, the United States took St. Augustine from the Spanish. The area was especially desirable for access to the ocean and its warm, sunny climate, thought to be curative for those with illnesses. But the handover from the Spanish left St. Augustine dirty, damaged, and overcrowded, perfect conditions for an epidemic.

Yellow fever hit the town incredibly hard. It was so bad that churches stopped ringing their bells to announce a death. If they hadn't, the bells would have been ringing their ghostly melodies night and day. But the cemetery's records only show three burials that entire year of the epidemic. In fact, there are hardly any headstones in the cemetery from between 1821 and 1835. So what happened to all of yellow fever victims from 1821? And all the other dead from the years after that? It may not be as sinister as it sounds.

Wooden grave markers cost less so they were a popular option back then. It's likely these low-cost markers marked the final resting place of many yellow fever victims, especially if multiple people in a family died at the same time. Those markers would have long rotted away. But many victims and families probably didn't have markers at all. If many family members died from yellow fever, the survivors wouldn't have been able to afford gravestones. Sadly, it was also common for people of color to be buried without markers, no matter the circumstances.

Another issue could be a factor. Before the cemetery had iron gates, people stole the wood fence posts for firewood. Although it sounds ghoulish, they probably even took the grave markers. So who knows where the actual boundaries of the cemetery lie? Think about it. With so many dead from yellow fever, all in one year, space was limited. And without a fence to mark the edge of the graves, it's not surprising that people would be buried wherever someone could find space. Yet another reason to be mindful when you're walking around St. Augustine. You never know who you might be stepping on!

O.C. White's Seafood and Spirits

Food and Spirits

You've read about some of the ghosts of St. Augustine pulling pranks on tourists and locals, but some ghosts take it too far. Keep that in mind if you visit O.C. White's Seafood and Spirits for a meal. The ghosts there are definitely not as friendly as others in town. Some of their pranks are just annoying, like candles being lit again after a waitress blows them out or stacks of chairs being taken apart.

But the restaurant's ghosts have a bad habit of pulling glasses off the shelves and throwing them at people. Some of the staff have even been injured. Plus, there's a lot of broken glass around.

Most of the paranormal activity happens in the middle of the night when the dinner guests have already left. But employees who work late have seen ghostly figures moving around the restaurant. Some of this activity has even been captured on film. One of the employees has a picture of the stairwell covered in mist. In that mist, you can clearly see the original owner, who built the house in 1791.

It's hard to dismiss stories about the ghosts of O.C. White's when so many people have witnessed spooky, unexplainable things there. An employee at the motel next door used to walk between the two buildings late at night. One day he smelled smoke and heard taps on the windows of the second floor of the restaurant, long after it had closed for the night.

Dave White, the current owner of the building, has also experienced paranormal activity such as candles lighting by themselves, weird smells, and glasses moving on the shelves. But the creepiest things seem to happen when he's alone or with only a few employees. Footsteps move across the second floor when no one is there. Salt and pepper shakers dance on the tables to some silent music only the ghosts can hear. There's even a door on the third floor that locks and unlocks itself.

Could you handle being there by yourself with all that going on? Even the most courageous ghost hunter has to think about that for a minute.

The Ghost Bar

Scarlett O'Hara's Bar sits in part of an old house that was once used as a funeral parlor, so you know ghosts just have to be lurking around every corner. After all, they don't call the upstairs "the Ghost Bar" for nothing! At least the ghosts there won't throw things at you!

George Colee was the owner and builder of the house in the late 1800s, and if you talk to any of the restaurant's employees, you'll learn he haunts the upstairs bar. The story goes that George drowned in the bathtub upstairs where the men's restroom is now located. He'd gotten into a fight not long before, so some say he might have been murdered by the other man. Or he could have just died in the bathtub. No one knows for sure. But George's presence in the building can't be denied.

The bathtub George died in stayed in the restaurant for a while, but it's not there anymore. It was repurposed as a sofa at one point. It also served as a salad bar, if you can

believe it. Can you imagine eating salad kept in a bathtub, much less a bathtub in which someone died? Gross!

You can still check out the bathroom, though. You'll have to climb a steep set of stairs to the second floor. They might creak as you go, warning you to turn back. But you won't listen, because ghosts are what you seek.

You won't actually *see* George, but you might feel him tap you on the shoulder or blow on the back of your neck. He likes to sneak up behind men using the urinal, so use the restroom before you get there!

Make sure to check out the portrait of George hanging on the wall upstairs. It's lit up by a small light on the edge of the frame. The portrait shows him as a young man, with hair parted down the middle and a sour expression on his face. You'll notice a rip in the canvas running across his face. Employees say it widens and narrows from day to day. They haven't figured out the reason, but they do know that George likes his image hanging in a certain spot so he can see people come in. If it's in the right spot, the portrait stays on the wall. Anytime employees move it from that spot, they'll find it on the floor later. It doesn't matter how many screws they use to hang it, it never stays on the wall.

His portrait isn't the only thing old George is picky about. He likes candles to be lit, and he wants napkins fanned out on the tables. If the employees don't do these things, he'll do them himself! This is why the restaurant doesn't put candles upstairs anymore—because George lights them when no one is around to put them out! He also dislikes cursing, like so many ghosts in St. Augustine. Once, he even shoved a police officer who was using some salty language. But if you're respectful, he'll leave you alone.

Employees warn of another ghost at Scarlett O'Hara's, but not much is known about him. This thin, dark man stalks the dining room, looking for something. Day or night, you'll find him there, searching for whatever he lost.

The Ghost Bar is a great place to go if you want a relatively safe ghost encounter. Just don't curse in front of George.

CHAPTER 8

Believe It!

You might think you've already seen everything spooky St. Augustine has to offer. But we're just getting started. Inside an old residence designed to look like a castle, there's a museum of all things weird and unexplainable. It's said to be the most haunted building on the Southeast coast, so it seems like a good place for us to look for paranormal activity.

Employees at the Ripley's Believe it Or Not! Museum will tell you all about the creepy things that happen after dark. Some of the resident ghosts like to turn the lights on and off when no one's around. Others like to play with exhibits that include music or recorded messages. The volume on these machines will go up and down by itself. Skeptics laugh and say the building is just old so the electrical wires don't work so well. But you and I know better. Are the ghosts bored and looking to scare people, or are they just as curious about the museum's odd contents as you are? You'll have to ask them when you visit.

You may have been to a Ripley's museum when traveling with your family. This museum has locations all over the world, full of strange and creepy things you might never have seen before. The St. Augustine museum even has a car made out of bones! But it's also special, because it might be the only museum that actually has documented ghosts. Visit there, and you can even put your ghost hunting skills to the test. Museum staff will teach you how to use all the ghost hunting equipment you see on your favorite paranormal shows. You'll learn about spirit boxes, devices used to communicate with spirits. They'll show you how special infrared thermometers will let you locate hidden ghosts in the room based on their temperature and then how to use cameras to capture photos of the ghosts. You'll even get to check out special recording devices that can capture the sounds made by ghosts called electronic voice phenomena (or EVP for ghost hunters like you).

The Ripley's building, originally called Castle Warden, has plenty of potential ghosts to meet if you visit. A rich oil man,

William Warden, built the enormous house in 1887 to hold his family of sixteen. Can you imagine that many people in your house all the time? But the family left the house vacant. Some destructive people took advantage of the fact that no one took care of the house. It fell into disrepair. Eventually, the city stepped in and planned to burn it to the ground, but a famous author bought it and, like many old buildings in St. Augustine, turned it into the Castle Warden Hotel.

In 1944, a big fire broke out in two rooms, with one on the third floor and one on the fourth. Two women supposedly died during the fire, but the strange circumstances have led to lots of theories about the fire covering up at least one murder. One victim had only been a guest of the hotel for less than two hours before the fire. The other victim had borrowed the owner's apartment on the fourth floor for a short stay because she was fighting with her husband.

Some say a burning cigarette in Room 17 on the third floor started the fire. According to the story, the person staying in that room asked a hotel employee to help. He left to get a fire extinguisher, but by the time he got back, the fire had spread to the owner's penthouse, where her friend was staying. Guests and employees heard screams, but they couldn't help. Flames licked the walls of the hallway, and ugly black smoke made it impossible to breathe. They had to leave it to the firefighters, who arrived too late.

The firefighters broke down the doors to the two rooms and found the women. The official cause of death was from breathing in the smoke. But what kept them from leaving their rooms when they smelled the smoke and saw the fire? The woman in Room 17 was found curled up in her bathtub. The woman upstairs laid on the floor of the bathroom.

There are rumors that the fire was set to cover up a murder. That may or may not be true, but we do know that the spirits of these women haunt the former Castle Warden.

Several rooms near where they died show a high level of paranormal energy. The museum has old-fashioned photo machines in the area. Visitors trying to use them often report being pushed out of the way by unseen hands. Maybe the women don't like tourists taking pictures of the place they died.

When these women appear, you'll see them standing at an upstairs window. Many report smelling smoke, even when nothing is burning. Others feel cold spots or have chills when they enter the area where the women died. Unfortunately, they took the mystery of what happened with them to their graves, and a killer may have gone free.

The Spanish Military Hospital Museum

CHAPTER 9

A Bloody History

It's hard to avoid ghosts in the Spanish Military Hospital Museum. Many soldiers died here, so it's not surprising a few hung around. Employees here will tell you that you can't work at the Museum without having a ghostly experience. One person who works here called it a "certified haunted building." That means it's the perfect place for us to visit next.

The Spanish Military Hospital was first hospital built in St. Augustine, and it only helped sick, wounded, or dying soldiers. This was during the early 1800s, when the Spanish still occupied St. Augustine. Because medical care wasn't like it is now, as many soldiers probably died from the conditions in the hospital as died from their wounds. Take a tour, and you'll hear more than you wanted to know about the bloody, brutal practices of the doctors. Soldiers even had their limbs cut off without any anesthesia, so they experienced all of it. You can imagine how the pain and fear of these men practically seeped into the very walls!

One area in particular has more paranormal activity than others. Those soldiers about to die were sent to a mourning room separate from the others. But it wasn't a peaceful place to spend your final hours. Patients had to listen to the sounds of saws and hammers making their very own coffins in the same room where they lay dying.

The existing building was reconstructed on the site of the original hospital, so you'd think it wouldn't be haunted. But the ghosts don't care. Everything that happened there didn't change just because the structure did.

There's something else about the old hospital that makes haunting a given. In the 1970s, when repairing a water line, city workers found more than they bargained: the

cobblestone street outside the old hospital covered up a mass grave. They found hundreds of skeletons and amputated limbs under the street. Bones of arms, legs, and feet scattered over the intact bodies of the dead. The workers didn't know what to do but cover the grave back up. In fact, you walk right over their remains as you enter the museum. But you and I both know their spirits aren't resting in the mass grave anymore.

Among all those soldiers is a nurse who can't let go of what she witnessed there. Some have seen her stalking the halls, dressed in her white nurse's uniform. Maybe she's haunted by something she did, or perhaps she just lost one too many patients to be at rest.

It's not surprising that many of the ghosts that haunt the halls of the old hospital are angry and want attention. After all, a lot of them died in agony and in brutal ways. The ghosts can get pretty physical when they want to make themselves known. Beds move around on their own. Crucifixes fly across the room. Strange noises in the building seem to be the least of your problems when you visit here!

If you go on a ghost tour at the hospital, you'll visit many of the rooms where these strange things have happened. You'll hear tales of the soldiers who died there and the spooky encounters over the years. It's a great place to get your ghost fix, for sure. But be careful what you wish for. One guest was saddened by the stories and asked if any spirits lingered in a room she visited. She got her answer when she returned home. On her back, the word "yes" had been imprinted into her skin. It faded away after she went back to the museum to show them, but I bet she didn't sleep well for a long time after that!

Flagler College

A Haunted Education

It's probably no surprise that the best-known place in St. Augustine is also the most haunted. But Flagler College—formerly the Hotel Ponce de Leon—has a lot more ghosts than your average haunted spot.

The hotel was built in 1895. It was one of the first buildings in the United States to be wired for electricity throughout. Can you imagine a time before electricity? It wasn't that long ago, when you think about it.

The hotel rooms now have been converted into dorm rooms for students at the college. So many people have passed through the doors of Flagler College since it was built, so you'd expect a lot of ghosts. But oddly, the only ghosts anyone sees are from when it was the Hotel Ponce de Leon.

Henry Flagler, the owner and builder, strolls the hallways and the dorms of the college. You never know what mood you might find him in, though, so beware! He has no respect for privacy and barges into student's rooms. They'll often find him standing at the foot of their beds when they wake up! But Henry also put his mark on the building, just in case you forget who created it. A distorted version of his face is etched into a small tile to the left of the entrance's main doors. Every time you walk in and out of the building, there he is.

His wife, Alice, is also lurking about. She stares at a spot on the wall where a portrait of Henry used to be. She could just turn around and see the man she loved, but it probably wouldn't be a happy reunion. You see, Henry's girlfriend also haunts the college. She died by suicide on the fourth floor of the girls' dormitory. Many have spotted her body hanging from the chandelier where she died. Unfortunately, you won't be able to spot her yourself if you visit. The college has closed the area to visitors.

Aside from the known ghosts, two unknown spirits linger in the halls of Flagler College. One, a ten-year-old boy, runs around annoying female students. The other is a lady in blue whose only quirk is bumping into the furniture. A lot has changed since she was alive.

Many students claim they haven't seen anything spooky here. Even some longtime employees say they don't believe the college is haunted. But the stories keep piling up. A lot of students who have seen ghostly apparitions don't talk about it. But they will tell you that the college has banned even students from going up to the fourth floor where Henry's girlfriend died. Others are happy to spill all the spooky tales of Flagler College.

One local says that during her sophomore year in the dorms, she was almost asleep when she felt something pressing down on her chest. Her roommate wasn't home, and she didn't see anyone in the room. She felt breath on her neck and heard someone whisper, "Come play with me." The words were repeated over and over.

She froze. She didn't know what to do and was more scared of getting up than remaining in bed with the whispers in her ear. The next day, she told the woman who monitored their dorm about the experience. The woman said her room was in the spot where the little boy died. He'd been upstairs playing with a ball that fell over the railing. He went after it, falling to his death on the first floor, just outside her room.

A local bartender tells a story about the little boy, too. The bartender's girlfriend woke up in her dorm room with a face hovering right above her. She had bruises on her legs. When she asked a local historian about ghosts at the college, he told her to watch for the little boy because he likes to bother the girls and pinch them.

I don't know about you, but stories like those would make me think twice before living in the dorms! Who wants to wake up to find a ghost watching you sleep, especially if they're going to pinch you?

CHAPTER 11

Punishment That Fits the Crime?

So far, most of the ghosts we've encountered haven't been so bad. They mostly just lurk around and pull pranks. But the ghosts who haunt the Old Jail in St. Augustine are a different breed. The conditions at the jail were terrible. Some of the most dangerous criminals in town were imprisoned there. Are you ready to meet some of them?

Tours of the Old Jail are popular for good reason. There are plenty of ghosts to meet. As one former tour guide said, ghosts are an occupational hazard if you work in St. Augustine. Because of the brutal, inhumane conditions at the jail, many prisoners died there. Some didn't last a year into their sentence before something happened to them.

Kim, one of the former guides, says rainy days bring out the best conditions for ghost-spotting. Especially the kind of rain that's so strong it scares you. Imagine lots of lightning streaking across the sky and thunder shaking the very ground under your feet. On days like that, the ghosts can't help but show themselves. Kim was so used to it that even the strangest happenings didn't make her blink. One day she noticed a man with a shaven head exit the cellblock where no one was supposed to be. A few minutes later, the iron door slowly creaked shut by itself—a door that weighs sixty-five pounds.

Looking at the Old Jail, you wouldn't guess what lies within. The pink exterior and architectural design make it look like a hotel. That makes sense if you know a little about St. Augustine's history and its most famous resident. Henry Flagler, who you met over at Flagler College, didn't want something so ugly in "his" town. It's a small town, after all, and his fancy guests paid for experiences that didn't include walking past ugly buildings that housed criminals. He demanded city officials move the jail from the planned location, but they would not. So Henry not only paid to make it look better than any other jail you've seen, but he also paid to have it built as far away from his beautiful hotel as possible. It's exactly one mile from the now Flagler College, the outer limits of St. Augustine at the time.

Inside the Old Jail, though, conditions were uglier and darker than you could imagine, even for a jail. Critters scrambled across the floor, looking for crumbs that didn't exist. Few windows let in light and air, so the place was always damp and smelled like mildew and sweat.

The jail had no running water. Getting a bath was a once-a-month thing, and all the inmates bathed in the same tub of water. After a month of living in the dirty jail and not bathing, that water would have been filthy after the first to use it. Can you imagine what it was like for the last one in line? What's worse is that the men had to do hard labor on a farm every day, so you know they stank. The few female prisoners had only two cells to share, and they did all the labor of cooking, cleaning, and laundry. They probably smelled just as bad as the men! If you visit the jail, you might get a whiff of one of them. That's probably a smell you'll never forget!

The punishments for the prisoners were also especially cruel. Sheriff Joe Perry ran the jail with a fierce determination from the time it opened in 1891. But his attitude wasn't the only thing that made him intimidating. The sheriff was three hundred pounds—mostly muscle—and towered over the prisoners. You didn't want to get him on your bad side if you could help it. He was so brutal that even minor slip-ups by the prisoners earned harsh punishments.

He often put convicts in the stockade for twenty-four hours. You might know what those are from the movies, but basically, they're big slabs of wood with holes for the head and hands. The stockade locked prisoners in place in a bent-over position, so they couldn't move. They couldn't sit or take the pressure off their legs. It would be uncomfortable from the beginning. After an hour or two, the prisoner would start to feel some pain. You can imagine what shape they'd be in after twenty-four hours.

Another similar punishment was called "the bird cage." This life-size cage was hung over a tree branch. The prisoner stood inside, dangling in the air until the sheriff decided to let him down.

But both of those punishments might have been better than the alternative. At least with those, the prisoners got to be outside breathing fresh air. If the sheriff sent you to solitary confinement, you were trapped in a room with no windows and no light and chained to the floor. Rats and cockroaches would be your only company. It's not like they'd let you out for a bathroom break.

Prisoners died from the punishments sometimes, of course. But many of the dead at the Old Jail died at the gallows. St. Augustine's Old Jail was what's known as a hanging jail, where men sentenced to die lived until their scheduled hangings. If you visit, you'll see a replica of the gallows, a wooden platform where the sheriff would string up nooses to put around the prisoners' necks.

Prison records say only eight men died on the gallows, but you probably wouldn't be surprised if I told you that there were some "off the record" hangings as well. It was an effective way to keep prisoners in line. Sheriff Perry made them watch the hangings as a warning.

Because of what the prisoners went through (or maybe just because it's dark), nighttime is the best time to experience the paranormal activity at the jail. The ghostly prisoners moan and wail in their former cells, still confined to the jail after all this time.

Before you feel too sorry for them, though, remember who we're talking about. One of the former prisoners who still lurks around sliced his wife's face with a razor blade. These men were the worst of the worst, condemned to die for their crimes. Maybe spending eternity in the prison is a fair punishment. Maybe it's too harsh. Luckily at the end of your ghost tour, you'll get to leave the cellblock. For them, death was the only way out.

St. Augustine Lighthouse

CHAPTER 12

A Light in the Darkness

You wouldn't still be reading if you didn't believe in the supernatural, and the St. Augustine Lighthouse is one of the best places in town to experience all things spooky. Now a museum, the lighthouse has many ghostly tales to tell. You might not be able to visit under the light of the full moon—the best time to go—but let's take the 219 stairs to the top and see who we encounter along the way.

Former lighthouse keepers always have the best ghost stories. Since they live and work at the lighthouse, they experience everything. One keeper recalled walking from the tower to the keeper's house one dark night and hearing the crunch of gravel behind him as if someone were following him. But no one was there. He had no shortage of other stories too, including one involving pigeons.

If you know a little about lighthouses, you know that pigeons can be a problem. They're drawn by the warmth of the lights and make their nests inside. You can imagine how gross it can get with pigeons making their home there! So, workers place special blocks to keep them out but still allow the light to escape. But one group of workers encountered more than pigeon poop. While installing these blocks, they looked up and saw a ghostly body hanging front the ceiling!

Tour guides and museum employees will tell you all kinds of stories. It's up to you to determine if they're real or not. You'll hear of ghostly hands reaching through doors and hearing someone singing when no one is there. Ghost detection equipment is said to light up in certain areas. Chairs have moved around on their own during tours.

The most famous story, though, begins around the time the lighthouse tower was replaced. Beach erosion had taken its toll through the years, and the original coquina lighthouse stood too close to the water. The city officials knew the tower would soon be engulfed by the ocean. A man named Hezekiah Pittee was charged with constructing a new tower—the same striped building you see today. In 1871, Hezekiah brought his family to

St. Augustine. He had four children, ranging in age from four to fifteen.

As the lighthouse tower was built, workers used a cement cart to transport construction materials. The cart was about two hundred yards long! It traveled on a rail, so workers could directly unload materials that came in on cargo ships. They then pulled the cart to the construction site to unload. The system used a gate at the water's edge to stop the cart from moving forward.

Construction sites are dangerous places, especially when you have a cart that's double the length of a football field! On July 10, 1873, Hezekiah's kids found out just how dangerous it could be. Along with a ten-year-old friend, they piled into the cart and rode it down to the gate at the water. But the gate didn't stop it. The heavy cement cart flipped, pinning the children under it.

One of the workers managed to rescue Hezekiah's two youngest children, but he couldn't save the others. In spite of the tragedy, Hezekiah finished the job and left with the rest of his family. But the three girls who died that day remained.

People see them frequently, not only at the lighthouse, but also hanging around the neighborhood in their old-fashioned clothes. There's a park with swings across the street, and if you grab a spot, you might find one of the girls swinging next to you. Maybe she'll dare you to swing harder and higher, or maybe she'll just laugh and move on. People see the

girls in the lighthouse sometimes too, and they've even tied visitors' shoelaces together as a prank!

After so many years with only each other to play with, the girls are ready for new friends. Maybe they'll let you chase them around the grounds. You'll know they're around even if you can't see them. Listen for their voices in the air, singing, whispering, and giggling. But don't hang out with them too long, or they might just try to keep you with them permanently!

End of the Line

Sadly, our ghostly walk through St. Augustine has come to an end, but we've only scratched the surface. There's a lot more to explore in America's most haunted city. Now you have a bit of a map to get you started on your own ghostly adventures.

While most places in St. Augustine have stories to share, there are a few that don't seem to have spooky tales waiting to be told. But in a city this old, the dead are all around, and they all have something to say.

Some of them just might not be ready to tell their truths yet. It can wait. They're not going anywhere, after all. One day, maybe when you've gone back one last time to the city gates, you'll find Elizabeth dancing with a new partner. Or you'll walk down the alley next to

O.C. White's and spot an unfamiliar shadow in the window.

Considering how often hidden graves are discovered in St. Augustine, there's always someone new to meet. They're waiting for you in the mist, just after dark when the moon is full. Don't forget your flashlight. And no cursing, just in case.